WHEN I GROW UP...

This book donated to Blair Ridge by Mrs. Hope, Administrative Assistant, from school opening in 2009 to 2023.

This book written by my sister-in-law Laura.

Enjoy

Mrs. Hope

Laura Forbes
When I Grow Up...

Illustrated by Catherine Campbell

Published by BooxAi

ISBN: 978-965-578-023-9

BooX AI

WHEN I GROW UP...

LAURA FORBES

Always Reach For The Stars ☆☆

Laura

This book is dedicated to all my great nieces and nephews and to my three great grandsons Adrian, Azia and Forest. You can grow up to be anything you chose to be, and whatever you chose, make it something that makes you happy and fulfilled.

When
I grow up I'd like to be;
A Pirate on the deep blue sea.
With everyone afraid of me,
BUT...
Can I bring my bear with
me?

A
Doctor! That's what I would
like to be. Saving lives in my surgery.
My mom would be so proud of me,
BUT...
Can I bring my bear with
me?

Perhaps
a Fireman is what I'd be. No
one would be as brave as me,
fighting fires; One, Two, Three,
BUT...
Can I bring my bear with me?

Maybe
an Actor is what I'll be. I'll be in
movies or on T.V. and be so
famous you'll all know me,
BUT...
Can I bring my bear with
me?

Or
a Pilot! That's what I could
be, flying over land and sea. You
would all want to fly with me,
BUT...
Can I bring my bear
with me?

A
Policeman! Yes! That could
be me, chasing the robbers up a
tree. Bad guys would run away from
me,
BUT...
Can I bring my bear with me?

There is so much that I could be. When I am grown, just wait and see!! I'll bring my bear, he'll stay with me 'cause I love him and he loves me.

Made in the USA
Middletown, DE
29 August 2022

72632259R00015